VIRGINIANA

A VISITORS' GUIDE TO VIRGINIA HISTORY & OTHER STUFF

Carolyn & Charles Bruce

Published by Hen a'Peckin' Press
a division of Bruce & Bruce, Inc.

Virginia Beach, Virginia

A Hen a'Peckin' Press Book
Published by Bruce & Bruce, Inc
Copyright © 2005 by Carolyn Bruce and Charles Bruce
Written by Carolyn Bruce and Illustrated by Charles Bruce
All rights reserved under the International and Pan-American Copyright Conventions

Bruce&Bruce
PUBLISHERS

Manufactured and Published in the United States by Bruce & Bruce, A Virginia Corporation
PO Box 64007, Virginia Beach, VA 23467-4007   www.VirginianaBooks.com
Distributed in the United States by BookMasters, Inc., Ingram, and Baker & Taylor
ISBN 0-9721674-4-7

This book is written with a two-fold purpose: one, to be entertaining, and two, to be historically accurate. The writer has used multiple sources from which to gather facts, and if mistakes were made they were inadvertant. However, our *opinions* are as valid as anyone else's. The illustrator did whatever he pleased, as he usually does.

Hen a'Peckin'
PRESS
2 0 0 5

INTRODUCTION

As the author and the illustrator of this book, we thought it would be great to have a history book about our home state, where our families have lived since colonial times and even before. In a way this is a story about our extended family, the Commonwealth of Virginia in all of its changes throughout the approximately 400 years the land has been called Virginia.

We also thought it would be fun to have the illustrations be humorous. As vast and as interesting as the history of Virginia is we have, by design, only a small space in which to tell the various stories, leaving many on the "cutting room floor." If any of the pages piques your interest, you'll be able to find out more on the Internet or in your local library.

We hope every reader will enjoy our book and learn about Virginia in this new and different presentation.

Carolyn and Charles

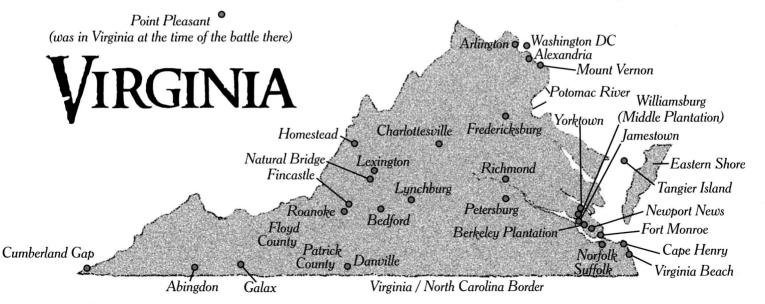

Point Pleasant
(was in Virginia at the time of the battle there)

VIRGINIA

Arlington · Washington DC
Alexandria
Mount Vernon
Potomac River
Williamsburg
(Middle Plantation)
Yorktown
Jamestown
Homestead
Charlottesville · Fredericksburg
Eastern Shore
Natural Bridge
Lexington
Fincastle
Richmond
Tangier Island
Lynchburg
Petersburg
Newport News
Roanoke
Berkeley Plantation
Fort Monroe
Bedford
Floyd County
Cape Henry
Patrick County · Danville
Norfolk
Virginia Beach
Cumberland Gap
Suffolk
Abingdon · Galax
Virginia / North Carolina Border

Welcome to Virginia, y'all!

First settled by the Engli… uh, the Scot… uh, the Indi…

First settled by the American native peoples before the end of the last ice age, Virginia is known for its hospitality, its mild climate, its beautiful vistas, its charm, and its history. We have often been invad… uh, overru…uh, visited… by folks from many other cultures, most notably the "Lobster Backs" and the "Blue Bellies." But, being true Southerners we warmly welcomed all (some have been received more warmly than others) to our Chesapeake and Atlantic shores, our mystical Blue Ridge, and our broad, rolling Piedmont Plateau.

It's All Mine, I Do Declare

--James I, King of England and VI of Scotland

VIRGINIA IN 1606

VIRGINIA TODAY

After several failed English attempts at colonization of this new land, some Englishmen chartered a business venture called the Virginia Company to try again. They aimed to get rich off the gold and gems laying on the ground here.

Before you laugh and say, "There's neither gold nor gems in Virginia!", look at this map. King James declared that his Virginia covered a swath from sea to sea and from latitudes 34 to 41 degrees N. (or, roughly from Cape Fear, NC to the northern point of Long Island, NY). That would take in all or parts of 22 of today's states, including Colorado's silver lodes and California's gold.

Of course, they couldn't know that then, nor could they have gotten to it if they had. Besides, the real gold in Virginia was its tobacco!

When the nearly naked native people just south of the Elizabeth River looked out to sea and saw European ships off the beach, they must have been frightened and angry. Who were these strangely dressed, pale-skinned men who were setting up a device made of wood on the water's edge? And what was this object, a signal? A hex? A weapon?

They watched as the foreigners knelt down and paid the thing homage. They decided to make the aliens leave, and attacked them with bows and arrows, and shouts and threatening gestures. The foreigners pointed their weapons which made fire and sounded like thunder. After that the warriors stayed well hidden behind the dunes, but while they watched, the odd men hastily got in their boats and left. The people rejoiced.

Our Jamestown Hero: John Smith

Captain John Smith came ashore under arrest at Jamestown and remained so for another two months. The expedition's leader, Captain Christopher Newport, had ordered Smith hanged for planned mutiny at sea and even had a gallows built in the islands, but instead kept him in the brig.

Smith's survival was perhaps a good thing, for when they opened their orders from London, they found he was named one of the council. Though he oft drew ire and rancor from his companions, he was apparently instrumental in preserving Jamestown by declaring that "he that will not work shall not eat" and by befriending (or abusing) and acquiring food from the local tribesmen.

Again threatened with a noose, Smith was saved by the timely return of Christopher Newport with fresh supplies. Yet, when he left Jamestown, he was as he arrived, in chains and unloved.

who knows the truth about pocahontas?

Before

After

Matoaka, daughter of Powhatan, was called "Pocahontas" meaning "wanton one" or "spoiled child". A little girl when the Englishmen arrived, her wont was to go to the English fort and play. After a while, she matured and the great chief Powhatan told her, "the English will catch you and eat you up..." if she continued going to the fort, but it didn't do any good. So, as Powhatan warned her, she was captured by the English, or she volunteered to be captured, and held at Henrico settlement.

White historians say she stayed there of her own accord... thus keeping her father from attacking the fort. The Indians tend to think she was forcibly held hostage, for the same reason.

John Rolfe, a big wheel at the fort (having developed a promising tobacco for the European market), told her if she ever wanted to get free, she must marry (English version: fell in love, asked her to marry) him. She did, and dressed English and was called "Lady Rebecca". They had a son after which the family went to England, met the king and saw the sights. But, at age 21, Matoaka grew ill and died. She is buried at Gravesend.

THE REAL FIRST THANKSGIVING IN AMERICA

Once upon a time, there was a fairy tale that the first "Thanksgiving" was held by the Pilgrims in 1621. Nay, nay, it be not so. Thanksgiving prayers first arose in 1619, in Virginia, and here, 1619 comes before 1621.

A group of 38 men from Berkeley Parish in Gloucestershire, England, arrived at a place along the James River on December 4, 1619 and, for having arrived safely in Virginia, proceeded to praise God. They established then that it was to be observed annually:

"Wee ordaine that the day of our ships arrivall at the place assigned for plantacon in the land of Virginia shall be yearly and perpetually keept holy as a day of thanksgiving to Almighty God."

Though we were not taught it in school, the fact remains that when the men from Gloucestershire set foot in Virginia and held what they conceived to be an annual observance of a day of thanksgiving, the Pilgrims were still in Leyden, Netherlands. Thus it is that Virginia rightfully claims origins of the national holiday we know as Thanksgiving, established at a place then in the wilderness, now Berkeley Plantation.

the Beginnings of middle plantation

In Europe there was no land available for an ordinary person, but Virginia had millions of acres. The Virginia Company used the lure of land to draw settlers to the colony providing fifty acres to any person who entered, or paid to bring another person, to the colony. Some transported whole families to Virginia and were suddenly land rich, but it was hard work to "improve" their new domains by felling trees, building homes, and clearing fields to grow crops.

One of those was Col. Thomas Ballard. Born in England in March 1630-31, he came to Virginia, marrying Anne Thomas in 1650. By importing at least 20 persons into the colony, he received a thousand acres of land, and over the years patented other sections. He was a prosperous, well-respected man, a Burgess, a Justice, and a Colonel in the Militia. Residing at "Middle Plantation", so called because it was middle-distance between Jamestown and Yorktown, Thomas purchased a nearby 330-acre tract which was sold in 1693 to the trustees of The College of William and Mary. There the school is sited today, as is much of Colonial Williamsburg. Being descended from Col. Thomas on two family lines, Charles Bruce just calls Williamsburg "Granddaddy's plantation"!

Welcome, Mister Warner. I'm Adam Thoroughgood. You, Sir, will be ancestor to the father of our country, George Washington, as well as to Robert E. Lee and Queen Elizabeth II. What do you say?

I say, what a Country!

At age 18, with few prospects in his native Norfolk, England, Adam Thoroughgood sold himself into servitude to have the opportunity to come to Virginia. By indenture, he was effectively a slave to Edward Waters, who "bought" him for the duration of the 1621 contract. He was obviously an exceptional man, for by 1635, he patented 5,350 acres of land on the Cheasapeakean River (which he renamed the Lynnhaven River after Kings Lynn, in Norfolkshire) for "special services and industries performed for the good of the colony."

The major part of his "services and industries" was the importation of 105 new settlers to Virginia under the "headrights" system, including a fellow named Augustine Warner, direct ancestor to George Washington, Robert E. Lee, and Queen Elizabeth II of Great Britain. Yep, all three.

Respected and admired by his community, Captain Thoroughgood is considered to be the earliest white settler in the area now within the City of Virginia Beach. The house that bears his name, however, was not built by him, as he died in 1640, and the house, perhaps the oldest brick house in America and certainly historic, was built about 1680 by his descendants.

Caribbean Entrepreneurs Set Up Shop at Cape Henry

Two decades after the settling of Jamestown, the Burgesses knew Cape Henry needed a lighthouse to guide ships into the bay, but, as governments are wont to do, they let a century pass before the subject was again mentioned. It was then decided that bonfires set on the cape would serve temporarily to guide the inbound ships. Without a hundred-year lapse, enterprising if murderous pirates often did away with the fires and those tending them, and set another fire farther down the beach. This caused ships to run aground, and the pirates then killed their crews and stole the cargoes.

BACON'S REBELLION

This has nothing to do with breakfast foods, but with bad weather, hard times, and short tempers in 1676. After a spate of wild weather and worsening economic problems, Nathaniel Bacon, a young cousin of the wife of Sir William Berkeley, Royal Governor of Virginia, led a raid against the local Indians, retaliating for an attack on a plantation. Wrong tribe. This led to worse attacks from the angered warriors. The governor tried to meet to have the settlers and the natives work things out, but instead, several chiefs were killed.

Bacon had support from some of the settlers and wanted to be made a "general" to lead troops against the tribes. Then things went awry entirely and Bacon laid siege to Jamestown. Bacon kidnaped the wives of prominent men, including those of the governor and Col. Thomas Ballard, and stood the women before his cannons in their white aprons to prevent being fired upon.

Frustrated that he was not achieving his aims, Bacon burned the town, and his men lost faith in him. He fled to Gloucester County where he died suddenly, but his body has never been found. Twenty-two of his men were hanged for their actions, and Governor Berkeley was recalled to England, where he died the next year.

Tobacco: The Savior of the Country

...Now...
Stick it in your
mouth and
set it on fire...

Jamestown was flagging. Industry after industry, from glassmaking to soap ashes, had been tried and found unprofitable. As an investment the colony was a failure.

Sometimes, however, fate takes a hand. In May 1609, a hopeful colonist named John Rolfe and his pregnant wife set sail on the *Sea Venture* in a convoy taking 500 settlers to Virginia. In a prime example of deus ex machina, a hurricane struck and the Rolfes' vessel was wrecked on a reef in the Bermudas, but all 150 aboard made it ashore.

For months they used parts of the wrecked ship and felled cedar trees to build two small ships they named *Patience* and *Deliverance*, to continue their voyage. Rolfe's wife had her baby daughter while there, but the baby, named Bermuda, died.

Reaching Jamestown after the "Starving Time", when all but 60 settlers died of starvation and disease, Rolfe was soon widowed. He poured his energies into experiments with some seeds he got in the Caribbean, and developed a sweeter, more palatable tobacco than that used by Virginia's Indians. Europeans could not abide the harsh native tobacco, though the variety Spain cultivated in her Caribbean colonies had become well accepted and the Spanish were only too happy to sell tobacco to English merchants for a premium price.

Rolfe sent a portion of his crop to England where it sold well. He met Pocahontas and in a while asked the governor for permission to marry the now Christian Indian maid. This they did in 1614, and the hostilities with the Powhatan tribe ended, at least long enough for the colony to expand and stabilize.

During this respite John took his family, now including a son, to visit England for several months. Tragically, Pocahontas, a.k.a. Lady Rebecca fell ill as they prepared to sail home, and before they had passed Gravesend, the lively girl of legend died and was buried there.

Rolfe was again bereft and, leaving his son in England with a guardian, returned to Virginia to continue his enterprise. He shipped ten tons of tobacco to England in 1617, and twice that the following year. By 1630, the total weight shipped was one and a half million pounds, but John Rolfe did not live to see it. He became a member of the House of Burgesses and married a third time to Jane Pierce. He died in 1622, perhaps in the massacre of whites in a surprise attack by the people of Pocahontas' tribe. Her father, Powhatan, had removed himself from power and society after her death.

In spite or because of the events surrounding his voyage to Virginia, John Rolfe had saved the colony from being an inglorious footnote to history. He arrived at a time when the colony needed a product to sell and make a profit. Out of all those in the convoy, his ship was the one that was wrecked, marooning him where he could get seeds for a better tobacco. Virginia's soil was ideal for growing it, and he had the ability to experiment with and improve the plants. His marriage to Matoaka gave the colony a number of years without warfare, when the planters could clear more land and grow more tobacco. (It is said the colonists eventually grew it everywhere, even in the streets of Jamestown.)

King James I of England & VI of Scotland, after whom Jamestown and the James River were named, abhorred the use of tobacco calling it "this vile custom of tobacco taking" and "a custom loathsome to the eye, hateful to the nose, harmful to the brain, dangerous to the lungs, and in the black stinking fume thereof nearest resembling the horrible stygian smoke of the pit that is bottomless." At that same time the leaf was becoming the most valuable commodity in the Commonwealth.

Tobacco came to be so valued as to be used instead of gold or silver as "current money of Virginia". People paid for goods and services with it. Employers paid salaries in tobacco. Even ministers received their annual stipend in a pre-established number of pounds of tobacco.

At first used "medicinally" for various ailments, tobacco was sniffed into the nostrils, chewed, carried in the mouth (dipped), smoked in a pipe, smoked rolled into "cigars," and it was applied as poultices.

It was not until Jacob Bonsack, a Virginian from Bedford County, invented the cigarette-making machine during Reconstruction after the Civil War, that tobacco became such an affordable and widely spread habit, especially in the era of World War I.

Once again, tobacco brought jobs and prosperity to Virginia.

(Right) In 1682 Nicholas Wise Jr., a shipwright, sold a 50-acre tract of land to trustees of Lower Norfolk County for ten thousand pounds of tobacco in cask. The land, to one day become the City of Norfolk, was bounded by the Elizabeth River, Back creek and Dun-in-the-Mire Creek.

THE FIRST COLLEGE CHARTER IN THE NATION

The Virginia Company's 1618 charter provided for a "University and College" to be established and plans were made for it, but with the Powhatans' uprising, and later the revoking of the Virginia Company's charter, royal favor was not forthcoming and the college was not built.

A second charter was granted in 1693, and the College of William and Mary opened a year later at Middle Plantation as an Episcopal school.

W&M was the first college to become a university, and survived though closed during the wars, in 1781 and the early 1860s, and hard financial times, in 1881 through 1887. Phi Beta Kappa (1776) came into being here, as did the honor system (1779) and the first school of law in the US (1779). W&M was first to offer studies in: fine arts, modern languages, modern history, and political economics. Three US presidents attended here (so far): Jefferson, Monroe, and Tyler.

The Wren Building, oldest academic building in continuous use in the US, is backdrop for a bronze (originally marble) statue of Norborne Berkeley, Baron de Botetourt. The first of the Royal Governors even to see the colony since 1705, he was a supporter of W&M and instituted the awarding of gold and silver medals to students of exceptional scholarship, awards still presented. After his sudden death in 1770, the well-loved Botetourt was memorialized with a statue... the first... and the only Virginia Royal Governor so honored.

A Magazine you can't Read...

Originally built in 1715, Williamsburg's brick Powder Magazine stands as a symbol, not only of the need for the colonists to defend themselves, but of the government's willingness to remove that ability when it so chose.

Royal Governor Lord Dunmore sent royal marines from *HMS Magdalen* on April 20, 1775, to spike the muskets and remove the stores of powder without which the Virginians could not rebel. But instead of making off with the vital explosive in secret, the marines were spotted and drums quickly alerted the city.

Angry Virginians gathered in the Market Square where several of their number convinced the mob to send Dunmore a demand that he explain his actions. He had, he said, received word that there was a "slave" insurrection afoot, and his action was to prevent the powder falling into their hands. He later admitted he had "Reason to believe the People intended to" seize the powder purchased for their defense, and he knew the colony's gunpowder equaled the colonists' power.

The following week word came of the Lexington and Concord battles, and by June 8th, Lord Dunmore fled the capital to take refuge on *HMS Fowey*, ending British colonial rule of Virginia.

Blackbeard hung out in Virginia

Blackbeard got his training serving aboard privateers during "Queen Anne's War" before joining a band of cutthroats. He soon captured a French slave ship, renaming her "*Queen Anne's Revenge*". Together they raged through the Caribbean and up the mainland as far as Delaware Bay for two years.

Virginia's Royal Governor Alexander Spotswood sent Lieutenant Robert Maynard with several sloops to put an end to the terror and the damage to Virginia's commerce.

Trapped at his homeport on the Outer Banks, Blackbeard put up a ghastly fight but was finally killed. His fearsome head, slung neath the bowsprit on Maynard's vessel, was brought back to Norfolk where it hung for years as a warning to other pirates, at "Blackbeard's Point" the confluence of the Hampton and James rivers in the Chesapeake Bay.

'Tis said his cranium was later made into a drinking cup.

Then, to quote one knowledgeable on the subject, the "skull was made into the bottom part of a very large punch bowl, called the infant, which was long used as a drinking vessel at the Raleigh Tavern in Williamsburg. It was enlarged with silver, or silver plated; and I have seen those whose forefathers have spoken of their drinking punch from it, with a silver ladle appurtenant to that bowl."

Eeeuw!

FRONTIER PEOPLE IN 1700s

By the 1700s the old matchlock guns were being replaced by flintlock muskets that needed no smoldering "match" to fire them.

Many frontiersmen wore slouch hats, but others preferred the dash and style (and availability in the wilderness) of the coonskin cap.

"Chaw"

Cotton or linen shirts used underneath, easier to wash in the pre-deoderant era.

Powder horn, made from a horn of an ox or other cattle, kept his critical powder dry and handy.

Buckskin (deerhide) clothing was serviceable and comfortable, adapted from the Native American style.

Shot pouch, carried small round lead balls and wadding.

Moccasins were in vogue, as were leather boots. Made to fit either the left or right foot, a shoe of that day was hard to "break in."

Indian "maid" for washin,' cookin,' and totin.'

Skinning knife for taking the fur off supper.

Dog

The Frontier of that day was any place west of Williamsburg

Feathers from eagles and other birds, worn ceremonially and to indicate bravery and tribal status.

Bow for shooting arrows at things too far away to clobber with a tomahawk.

Many eastern tribes were tattooed on their faces and other parts of their bodies.

Arrows, or small razor-sharp stones tied on the ends of sticks, used with bow for defense and hunting.

Indian "maid" for plantin,' weedin,' harvestin,' grindin,' tendin,' fetchin,' sewin,' beadin,' buildin,' washin,' cookin,' and totin.'

Steel bladed knife, acquired from whites to replace sharp stones.

Loincloth, soft skin or cloth worn by men and women to conceal the loins in summer. Way more modest than bikinis!

Steel bladed hand axe, acquired from whites to replace sharp stones tied on sticks (tomahawks).

Moccasins. Women of some tribes would chew the leather to make it soft for his comfort, some wearing their teeth down to the gumline.

She Floated into Virginia History

Pretty, wealthy (195 prime acres), a widow with three sons, a healer who knew about plants and herbs and midwifery, she was quite sensible, choosing to wear her late husband's breeches instead of women's clothes to work in the fields of her farm.

Her neighbors said she was a witch.

Grace White Sherwood was twelve times accused, investigated, and examined, and in 1706, agreed to a trial by water. With no ducking stool, the sheriff rowed her out into Lynnhaven Bay, tied her thumbs to her opposite big toes, and put her into the deep water clothed only in a sack.

If she sank and drowned, she was innocent, but if she floated or swam, she was a proven witch and could be hanged. Giving her every opportunity to be confirmed not a witch, the sheriff had thoughtfully tied a thirteen-pound Bible around her neck. But Grace untied her thumbs and the Bible and swam to shore, thus condemning herself.

Fortunately, she was not hanged but for years resided in the Princess Anne County jail. She was eventually released and her land was restored to her, leaving her Virginia's only "proven" witch.

Before her trial, she had warned the gathering crowd that they would be as soaked as she by the end of the day, and a sudden storm swept in to make her prediction come true...

the DIVIDING LINE BETWEEN NORTH VIRGINIA AND SOUTH VIRGINIA

OK JONES, YOUR TURN AT THE CHAIN

NORTH CAROLINA

VIRGINIA

In the 1660s, King Charles II gave half of Virginia to eight "proprietors" (cronies). South of today's Virginia, the lands included Georgia and the Carolinas and everything due west to the Pacific. Virginia, a crown colony, and the proprietorship had different rights and rules, and people began to push for a "dividing line" so that those near the border would know which way to jump.

Seventy years later the line was finally drawn, but by then all but one proprietor had sold back to the crown. Starting at a point on the sandy coast north of Currituck Inlet, representatives of both colonies surveyed 73 miles of swamps and forests in two months, quit for the summer and returned to plot another 100 miles that fall, and after the Carolinians went home, the remaining party carried on to the Appalachian foothills.

Virginia commissioner William Byrd II kept a journal in two versions, both published after his death. One he wrote for the public to read, the other (with more commentary) for friends. He was one of America's first authors.

WHO'DA THOUGHT HE'D BE PRESIDENT?

The father of our country was adventuresome and clever with "ciphering" as a young man, and turned those traits into a profession. At age 18 he was accomplished enough to survey properties for a number of his neighbors, including Lord Fairfax, for whom he surveyed Natural Bridge in 1750. His carved initials are still visible high along the wall above the creek.

Nearly a quarter-century later, the tract of land including Natural Bridge was bought by another future president, Thomas Jefferson, who built the first "guest cabin" there. At a height of 215 feet, the bridge is truly one of the world's natural wonders, sacred to the Monacan tribe.

Photo by the author

Williamsburg was begun as Middle Plantation, a working farm between Yorktown and Jamestown, 1600s.

Town chosen as the colony's capital in 1699.

Site of Dunmore's raid on the Virginia powder magazine, historic moves to independence, 1763-1779.

Relinquished as Virginia's capital, 1779.

Landing point for many of Washington's troops on the way to meet Cornwallis at Yorktown, 1781.

Quiet little village until the Civil War, when Union troops under General Hooker attacked the rear guard of the retreating Confederates under General Longstreet, May 5, 1862.

Sleepy little village until John D. Rockefeller, Jr. bought up much of the town's properties and founded The Colonial Williamsburg Foundation which recreated buildings that had been razed, restored buildings that had been altered, returned the town to how it must have looked as Virginia's capital, enabled visitors to look back in time, 1926 thru today.

Scene of re-enactions of Williamsburg's colonial daily life.

Williamsburg

The first Colonial Capital at Jamestown, Virginia laid claim to another "first" on July 30, 1619, when representatives of the various sections met in Jamestown's church to form a legislature. Until that day, no European colony in the Americas had any form of self-governance; all governmental matters were decided by the colonies' respective kings. Spain and France both had absolute monarchies.

England's kings, however, were restricted by the Magna Carta, signed in 1215 by King John granting English freemen rights the crown could not usurp. England's colonists were given charters that guaranteed that they would hold those same rights.

Upon his arrival in Virginia in 1619 the new governor, George Yeardley, lifted the martial law that had been in effect for years and declared that the settlers would thenceforth have their own version of the English Parliament. Like their fellow Englishmen at home, they would have a say in their government.

The House of Burgesses was comprised of men chosen by the various boroughs to represent their

america called a "capitol"

views and interests. Ultimately, it was hoped that more self-rule would create greater returns for the investors in London since the colony was then a profit-oriented settlement rather than a royal colony. Thus it was appropriate that the assembly's first action was to set a minimum price for tobacco.

In spite of an attempt by King James to dissolve the new legislature, the Virginians refused to give up their rights as Englishmen and continued to meet at least once a year to decide local issues. This did not bode well for the English kings, for every subsequently implanted colony also demanded an assembly. Some might say the seeds of independence were sown by the Virginians in that tiny church in Jamestown.

In 1698, after Jamestown burned for the third and last time, it was decided to move the capital to Middle Plantation (soon renamed Williamsburg). There the House of Burgesses assembled in the just completed Wren Building at the College of William & Mary, however, they had resolved the previous May to construct a new Capitol in their new home.

Henry Cary, builder of the Wren Building, also erected the Capitol, which was not completed until 1705. Haunted by the threat of fire, the Burgesses had the Capitol constructed without fireplaces; even candles and tobacco pipes were disallowed

inside! In spite of their caution, however, fireplaces were added in 1723 because the building was so uncomfortably cold and damp. Sure enough, the Capitol was gutted by fire in 1747.

Another Capitol of a much different style replaced it, and it was there, in 1765, that Patrick Henry introduced *The Stamp Act Resolves*, four of which were enacted by his fellow Burgesses. The first plainly sets forth the way Virginians felt about being taxed from London for the purpose of raising money:

Resolved, that the first adventurers and settlers of His Majesty's colony and dominion of Virginia brought with them and transmitted to their posterity, and all other His Majesty's subjects since inhabiting in this His Majesty's said colony, all the liberties, privileges, franchises, and immunities that have at any time been held, enjoyed, and possessed by the people of Great Britain.

Virginians still thought of themselves as Britains, and expected to be governed as such, but a decade later, the bond was broken beyond repair. Going into the trying years before the Revolution, Governor Dunmore, concerned that the burgesses were speaking their minds against the king, twice dissolved (1773, 1774) the assembly. It did not win him any supporters, and the Burgesses continued their deliberations by walking down Duke of Gloucester Street to the Raleigh Tavern, to meet there until readmitted to the Capitol.

Burgess Patrick Henry on March 23, 1775, spoke these most famous words: *Gentlemen may cry, peace, peace -- but there is no peace...Our brethren are already in the field! Why stand we here idle?... Is life so dear, or peace so sweet, as to be purchased at the price of chains and slavery? Forbid it, Almighty God! -- I know not what course others may take; but as for me, give me liberty or give me death!*

With the other English colonies, Virginia soon openly rebelled and the rest is... well, history.

Richmond, being accessible by water, was chosen as the new capital city in 1799, and the second Virginia Capitol gradually vanished. In 1928 Colonial Williamsburg acquired the site and by 1934, as closely as possible, reconstructed the 1705 Capitol we see and cherish today.

D. BOON KILT A BAR

Daniel Boone was born and lived until his mid-teens in an area of Pennsylvania near present-day Reading. In an age when a man's ability to hunt put food on the family table, the youth became a crack marksman and a renowned backwoodsman. His family moved to the Yadkin Valley of North Carolina where, about age 20, he joined militia in the French and Indian War. From the older men he heard stories of a place beyond the mountains, wild and mostly unexplored by white men.

After returning home he married a neighbor girl named Rebecca Bryan, but it wasn't long before the lands beyond the mountains beckoned and he was drawn time and again to the area of Virginia that is now Kentucky, sometimes staying gone for years. He acquired a reputation as a trailblazer and was hired to guide settlers into the land of the Bluegrass, where he left a legacy of several settlements and much lore.

In 1788, he went to the area of Virginia that would later become West Virginia, but before the decade was out he headed farther west in a dugout canoe. Asked why he was leaving Virginia, he said simply, "Too crowded."

As Far West As You Can Go In Virginia

Few folks realize that the Old Dominion stretches over 400 miles across. From the Eastern Shore on the Atlantic to deep in the rugged, forested mountains at a place called Cumberland Gap, Virginia goes farther west than is Detroit, Michigan.

The Native Americans had been following migrating herds through the gap for millennia, but the first European known to have made the trek was an indentured servant named Gabriel Arthur in 1674, and there were no doubt others.

Daniel Boone first slipped through the gap between mountains in 1769. Six years later, he went through again with a crew to blaze the trail, having been hired by Col. Richard Henderson's Transylvania Company, which wanted to settle the area for safety back home in NC, and, of course, profit.

Boone himself moved into Kentucky, and along with the hardy pioneers, founded Boonesboro and Harrodsburg, but he moved on after a while.

Today, a national park surrounds the gap, called the most significant mountain pass east of the Mississippi.

Not So Pleasant At Point Pleasant

In 1908, the US Congress declared that the first battle of the Revolutionary War was fought at Point Pleasant, Virginia, October 10, 1774, when the western Virginia militias were called out against the Ohio Indian tribes for causing trouble on the frontier, perhaps at Governor Lord Dunmore's instigation.

General Andrew Lewis, leading a thousand to twelve hundred men, was to join with Dunmore and another thousand, but Dunmore hadn't arrived when around a thousand warriors under Shawnee Chief Cornstalk attacked Lewis' camp at dawn and a horrendous battle raged.

The Indians then withdrew, having lost about 150 warriors. The Virginians' 200 casualties included Gen. Lewis' brother Charles, killed, and Col. William Fleming, badly wounded. Pursued by the newly arrived Dunmore troops, the Indians sued for peace, and "Dunmore's War" ended.

Within the year Dunmore was deposed and Lewis was sent to chase him out of Virginia, but by the Yorktown surrender in October 1781, Lewis had taken ill and died. Fleming survived his terrible wounds, but his injured arm precluded further military service. Still, he did many other things, including guarding the colony's powder, and serving as governor after Jefferson resigned and before Thomas Nelson took office.

LIGHTHORSE HARRY?

Of course Henry Lee was nicknamed, "Lighthorse Harry", he led a light cavalry troop! Besides, his cousin was named Francis Lightfoot Lee. It fit.

Born near Dumfries in 1756, Lee was from an already distinguished family. When relations with the king grew dicey, he joined Virginia's cavalry as a captain, transferring to the Continental army two years later.

There he rose in rank, first to major for his valor in combat, then to lieutenant colonel for his brilliantly successful raid on Paulus Hook (Jersey City), New Jersey in August 1779. Congress even gave him a gold medal.

He harried the troops of Cornwallis while under the command of Nathaniel Greene in the Carolinas, but retired from military service in 1781 due to ill health. Even so, he continued to serve, as a member of the Continental Congress, as Virginia's governor, as a US Congressman, and as a supporter of the Constitution.

When his great friend George Washington died, it was he who stood before the combined houses of Congress and eulogized the former president with the famous words: "First in war, first in peace, first in the hearts of his countrymen."

Lighthorse Harry Lee's reputation faltered after he had financial troubles. He died and was buried in South Carolina in 1818, and was reinterred beside his son, Robert E. Lee in Lee Chapel at Washington & Lee University.

Done More Bad than Good, He Did!

John Murray, Lord Dunmore, had a penchant for alienating the Virginians he had come to govern. He arrived in the colony in 1771 and proceeded to twice disband the Virginia House of Burgesses, start a war against the western Indians, seize the Williamsburg magazine's powder, abandon the governor's palace, take refuge on a British warship, declare martial law, close the press that criticized the king and the government, send troops to plunder Virginians' plantations and farms, get his troops whipped at Great Bridge, and on Jan. 1, 1776, bombard and burn to rubble Norfolk, the largest, most loyal-to-the-crown city in the colony!

Oh, I take that back. A couple of buildings survived the fires and explosions set off by the bombardment, one being St. Paul's Church, now in downtown but then on the northern edge of the city. Look closely and you will see a cannonball from Dunmore's attack, still lodged in the wall of the venerable structure.

THE VIRGINIA CONTINENTAL SOLDIER

He was required to have at least two opposing teeth so that he could bite the ends off the paper cartridges.

He wore a tricorn cockaded hat, usually black with a white trim. The cockade was sometimes a rosette and sometimes a sprig of evergreen.

His haversack carried everything he would need: tools to clean and repair his rifle, eating utensils, razor, etc. and weighed as much as 40 pounds.

His uniform coat was dark or navy blue with red facings and showing pewter buttons.

He usually wore a white or pale blue linen or cotton shirt and a white waistcoat.

His rifle could be American, French, or British and had a bayonet. Officers carried swords and pistols.

Cartridges, one round lead shot, and gunpowder wrapped in paper, were carried in his cartridge pouch.

He carried his own water in a wooden canteen

Drop-front breeches, made of wool or linen, were white or buff color, and tied in the back for a better fit.

Gaiters were sometimes part of the uniform, but some units wore white wool or linen stockings.

He stood about 5 feet 2 inches and weighed about 120 pounds. This was an average as General Washington was well over 6 feet tall as were many others. He could be as young as 12 or as old as 60.

Shoes were of leather, black or brown, with buckles, or sometimes laces.

The Declaration of Independence

Fifty-six brave men signed the Declaration of Independence; among them was Virginia's delegation: Richard Henry Lee and his brother Francis Lightfoot Lee, Carter Braxton, Benjamin Harrison, Thomas Jefferson, George Wythe, and Thomas Nelson, Jr.

Brave because each knew that if the Revolution failed, he would forfeit his wealth, his position, and his life, leaving his family destitute.

One of these was the first Professor of Law in America, though he was financially unable to complete law school. One was the third President of the United States. One put a bounty on his own home when Yorktown was under siege and Continental cannons were firing on the town. One was the father of one, and the great-grandfather of another, US President.

Several were governors of Virginia. Most were members of the House of Burgesses, Virginia's colonial legislature. Several lost fortunes by financially supporting the war. One wrote the Declaration of Independence and founded a major university. Many were abolitionists. One willed part of his family estate to his freed slaves, resulting in his being murdered by another heir. And four attended the College of William & Mary.

Signers Shown Here are Reenactors

A Giant With a Tall Order

George Mason was a giant. Not physically, but intellectually he was huge. He was the one who dreamt up Virginia's Declaration of Rights, which served as archetype for other documents like the Declaration of Independence and the Bill of Rights, the first ten amendments to the US Constitution.

George Mason was born in 1725 and "orphaned" at age 10. In that era, when a child's father died he was an orphan and needed an adult male to look after his interests. George was fortunate in that his uncle/guardian was a man with a large library, much of it concerning the law.

He married, had children, became more political, assumed various positions, like justice of the Fairfax County court, a trustee of Alexandria, and a Burgess. He helped compose the Fairfax Resolves against the Boston Port Act, and at war's end, he drew up papers in which Virginia ceded its western lands to the United States.

He went to the Constitutional Convention in Philadelphia and debated heartily, but in the end, he refused to sign the document because he saw problems: the federal benches would render state courts impotent, the wealthy would dominate the poor, and the government would become an oppressive monarchy or aristocracy.

George Mason died in 1792 and lies buried on the grounds of his home, Gunston Hall.

THE FRENCH CONNECTION

On July 16th 1781, French Admiral de Grasse received dispatches from generals Washington and Rochambeau requesting urgent aid in either New York or the Chesapeake Bay. Nearly a month later his reply reached Washington, and the "urgent" request being met at top speed, de Grasse anchored 24 ships of the line and two frigates off Lynnhaven beach the last of August.

Meanwhile the British fleet suffered delay upon delay and were September 5th getting to the Virginia Capes from Long Island with a total of 19 ships of the line and eight frigates. Their sails were spotted, and the French rapidly made ready and put to sea.

We could have stood in the dunes and watched the greatest sea battle of the Revolution, close off the coast of Virginia, between the vans of the French and the British, the rest of their fleets not effectively joining the fight. Finally, darkness called a halt.

For days the British tarried before having to sink one ship, and neither command forced another action, the British sailing back to Long Island. The French were able to blockade the Bay, precluding the naval rescue of Cornwallis and his command, and with more French troops than American, Washington held his siege until Cornwallis, his command out of food and supplies, surrendered.

SURRENDER!

Charles, Lord Cornwallis, had stood before the House of Lords and criticized the heavy tax burden his government laid upon its American colonies in the decade before the Revolution, but he could not abide their declaring independence. He volunteered to serve in America to put down the "rebels," only to find "The World Turned Upside Down"* at Yorktown, Virginia.

Wrote Dr. James Thacher, a witness to the British surrender, October 19, 1781, "...when it is considered that Lord Cornwallis has frequently appeared in splendid triumph at the head of his army, by which he is almost adored, we conceive it incumbent on him cheerfully to participate in their misfortunes and degradations, however humiliating; but it is said he gives himself up entirely to vexation and despair."

*Name of the tune said to have been played by defeated British troops while leaving the field of surrender.

The end that was the beginning

WAHHHHHHH!!

After the surrender ceremonies, General George Washington sent a message to the Continental Congress that began: *"Sir: I have the Honor to inform Congress, that a Reduction of the British Army under the Command of Lord Cornwallis, is most happily effected..."* But in truth, Washington was overjoyed; the "reduction" took out of action one-third of the British troops in America, ending the last major battle of the war.

The surrender terms were the same as the British had given after taking Charleston, SC, from Major General Benjamin Lincoln the previous year. Cornwallis was said to be ill and unable to attend the ceremony, thus his second-in-command, Brigadier General Charles O'Hara, surrendered Cornwallis' sword.

Purposely or not, O'Hara snubbed the Americans and offered it instead to French General Comte de Rochambeau, who pointed him toward General Washington. As was proper, Washington then sent O'Hara to surrender to his second-in-command, Major General Benjamin Lincoln.

A term of affection first applied to the Virginia Colony by England's King Charles II, who ruled from 1660-1685. He fled after his father was executed in 1649 and the Roundheads took over the government, but Virginia remained loyal to the crown. When Charles was restored to the throne, he recognized Virginia's unfailing support by quartering his arms to show Virginia among his other dominions: France, Ireland, and Scotland. Loyal Virginians were nicknamed "Cavaliers."

THE OLD DOMINION

King Charles II of England

A MOUNTAIN OF CONCEIT

Some of our North Carolina neighbors have referred to their state as "A valley of contentment between two mountains of conceit" (Virginia and South Carolina)!

THE MOTHER OF PRESIDENTS

As you read through this book, you'll find that, of the current total of 42* men who have served as US President, native Virginians have held the post eight times, more than any other state's sons: Washington, Jefferson, Madison, Monroe, W. Harrison, Tyler, Taylor, and Wilson.

*Grover Cleveland, born in New Jersey in 1837, is counted as the 22nd and 24rd presidents, having been elected to two non-consecutive terms in 1885 and 1893. Still, he was only one man, thus, the number 42.

THE MOTHER OF STATES

At one time, the Commonwealth of Virginia held claim to most of the Northwest Territory, including all or parts of Ohio, Indiana, Illinois, Michigan, Wisconsin, and Minnesota. These lands she ceded to the US in 1784 so that landlocked states in the east would ratify the Constitution. The several counties of Kentucky became a separate state in 1792, and West Virginia in 1863.

The Emperor of America?

There are numerous stories about George Washington. Most are untrue. The thing about the cherry tree? Made up story by Mason Locke "Parson" Weems, a minister who wrote often of Washington and his many virtues.

Washington's most notable virtue was, perhaps, that he refused to be the emperor of America. Devastated when the officers he had led through the Revolutionary War averred that he should become king of the newly formed country, he refused, saying that he had not fought to free his homeland from the British monarch only to replace him on the throne of an American kingdom.

As his second term as President of the United States was ending, the crown was again offered to the Virginian, and again he refused.

When told that the American president would refuse the offered throne, King George III, against whose armies Washington had so valiantly fought, is said to have gasped, "If he does that, he will be the greatest man in the world!"

Washington returned to his Virginia home, establishing precedent for the peaceful surrendering of power for future generations to follow. He died less than three years later and is buried beside his wife, Martha Ball Custis Washington, at Mount Vernon.

Alexandria

During the Civil War Virginia had three capitals, Richmond and Wheeling and Alexandria. "What?" you may ask. "How did Virginia manage to have three capital cities?"

Richmond, the capital since 1780, yet remained so, and had been selected by the Confederate States of America as its national capital. Some Virginians, however, wanted their state to remain within the US, and set up an alternative government in Wheeling, then in Virginia.

In 1863, after West Virginia was accepted into the Union as a separate state, Virginia's alternative government had to move to a place inside Virginia. Considering the availabilities, the Union Governor of Virginia, Francis H. Pierpont, chose the city of occupied Alexandria as his capital. Just across the Potomac from Washington, DC, surrounded by Union troops, it was surely well defended. Alexandria remained the alternate capital until Richmond was taken in 1865, and Pierpont became governor of the Commonwealth. A military commander was appointed three years later.

Actually, Alexandria in its early days had been given away. After the Revolution, a large tract including Alexandria had been ceded to the US for the establishment of a Federal District (later the District of Columbia). By the 1840s, most in the Virginia side of the district were wholly unhappy with the situation. In their minds, there were few benefits and some big drawbacks to living there. Why, they couldn't even vote! A few years before the Civil War the lands Virginia had ceded, including Alexandria, were returned to the Commonwealth.

Lucky James, He Married Dolley

Not an imposing figure, James Madison had a brilliant mind. Often called "The Father of the Constitution," Madison credited "many heads and many hands" with its birth.

Born in King George County, he grew up and lived all his life in Orange County, but graduated from the College of New Jersey (now Princeton). History, government, and law were his forte, and his country put his immense talent and intelligence to good use in the construction of The Virginia Constitution (1776). He served as delegate to the Continental Congress (1780-1783, 1786-1788) and the Constitutional Convention (1784), and was one of the authors of The Federalist Papers.

He served as Secretary of State under Thomas Jefferson and, when Jefferson's daughter Patsy gave birth (the first child born in The President's Mansion), her son was named James Madison Randolph.

The 4th man and the 3rd Virginian to be elected President of the United States, Madison was faced with Britain and France, at war with each other, raiding US ships, precipitating the War of 1812 (see Dolley Madison).

PERFECT! ALL THEY MUST DO NOW IS FOLLOW THE ———— DIRECTIONS!

George's Key to the Jail-House...

Mounted in a glass display case on the wall at Mount Vernon, in Fairfax County, is a heavy antique key. It's just an old key, not pretty, and its material is of little monetary value. Why would Washington have displayed it with such reverence? It is a long story.

In Paris, France, July 14, 1789, a rioting mob broke into the hated political prison known as the Bastille and threw open its doors, allowing all the prisoners to flee. From that spark flamed the French Revolution, and the Marquis de Lafayette was made Commander of the French National Guard. During his tenure he ordered the Bastille torn down, and in remembrance of, and respect for, his old friend and commanding officer in America, he sent one of the keys from the Bastille to Washington.

By then, Washington had been sworn in as the First President of the United States, and he displayed the key proudly on the wall in the Executive Mansion through his term of office. Then he took it back to Mount Vernon with him, where it remains.

In 1989, the bicentennial of the storming of the Bastille, the key was lent to the French government to use in their celebrations, a reminder of the time when French support for our own Revolution made all the difference in a little place called Yorktown.

Jefferson sold Lewis & Clark down the river...

A long revolution by insurgents in the French West Indies succeeded just when Napoleon had acquired the Louisiana Territory from Spain, leaving France with less purpose for the vast area. Thus it was that the US was able to strike a $15 million deal for its purchase (at about three cents an acre) with the needy French emperor late in 1803. The size of the US was instantly doubled.

President Thomas Jefferson, whose interest in the American West was so great that he owned more books on the subject than were in any other library in the world, sold Congress on the idea of sending Virginians Meriwether Lewis and William Clark to investigate and map the country's new lands and everything in them. And, oh yes, they should also find a Northwest Passage to the Pacific so the US would have access to the Orient.

Jack Jouett's Ride

On the lawn of The Cuckoo, a tavern my friend,
Lay Captain Jack Jouett a'catchin' a nap,
When Banastre Tarleton and his bloody men
Rode by to get Jefferson caught in their trap.

Jack knew where they headed and took to his horse,
To hie *forty miles* through dark forest and glen,
All night he rode hard and took many a course,
That beat him with brambles and slashed at his skin.

Monticello lay peaceful in wan light ere dawn,
He had beaten Tarleton to Jefferson's door,
And flying across the home's broad green fore lawn,
He roused up the household in few minutes more.

"Tarleton!" he cried as he gasped for his breath,
"He comes for you, Governor! Leave right away!
And if I've not ridden my horse to his death,
I'll ride down to Charlottesville, warn the Assembly!"

And off like a demon he rode in the morn,
To carry his message, the Assembly to wrest
From the hands of Banastre, the one they did scorn.
They left set for Staunton, away in the west.

He'd saved all Virginia had Jouett that night,
And Tarleton, Cornwallis and King George's pride
Fell to us at Yorktown, with a siege and a fight,
Which could not have happened, without Jouett's ride.

"millions for defense... not one cent for tribute!"

Native to Fauquier County John Marshall served with Washington during the Revolutionary War in PA, NY, NJ, suffering through the winter at Valley Forge. After hearing George Wythe lecture, Marshall chose law as his profession, and served in the Virginia House of Delegates where he helped get ratified the US Constitution.

He turned down appointments in the federal government until one as commissioner to improve the relations between the US and France was proffered.

Upon being told that French officials required bribes to look favorably on US matters, Marshall refused and the saying in the heading above was coined.

Elected to Congress from the Richmond District, he again spurned offers of higher positions including those of US Supreme Court Justice and Secretary of War, but he accepted a cabinet office under President John Adams. He was thereafter appointed Chief Justice of the US Supreme Court.

Before his death in 1835 he, more than any other, established the judicial branch of the government as co-equal to the legislative and executive branches.

DOLLY CUTS GEORGE OUT OF THE PICTURE

Born in Piedmont, North Carolina, Dolley Payne was the daughter of Quakers from Virginia. In her teens, she and her family moved to Philadelphia, at the time the national capital. There Dolley married John Todd, Jr., but several years later an epidemic left her a widow with a small son.

In 1794 she married James Madison, an older man and a Virginia Congressman who would be elected President in 1808. By then, Dolley was Washington's best known, best loved hostess, and it was she who held the first Inaugural Ball and first decorated the President's House. She held weekly "open house" parties, drawing all of Washington's powerful to her social functions.

All did not go well at the President's House during her tenure, however. In 1814, the natural stone mansion was one of the buildings in the path of the invading British. With little warning, Dolley and the staff gathered what they could, including (some say) cutting Gilbert Stuart's standing portrait of George Washington out of its frame in order to take it with them, and fled into Virginia.

When she returned, the house was blackened and gutted, and had to be totally rebuilt inside and painted outside before it was reopened. Due to its being painted, the President's House came to be called the White House.

He Drew a Line in the Sand... Uh, Sea!

Thomas Jefferson is said to have commented, "Monroe (is) so honest that if you turned his soul inside out there would not be a spot on it."

James Monroe was born in Westmoreland County in 1758 and was educated at the College of William & Mary. During the Revolution he served in the Continental Army, after which he became a lawyer in Fredericksburg.

His interest in politics led him to become an anti-Federalist. He was elected a US Senator in 1790, and was later appointed a minister to France, where he developed an affinity for the French, an advantage when he and Robert Livingston negotiated the Louisiana Purchase.

In 1816 and again in 1820, he was elected President of the US. During his administration the Missouri Compromise postponed the destruction of the US for another generation, and in foreign affairs, Spain was preparing to colonize parts of Latin America. Both the US and Great Britain opposed Spain's plan, but Monroe and his Secretary of State, John Quincy Adams, realized the US must make its stand alone.

Thus the Monroe Doctrine was born. In essence it said that the Americas were free and independent, and that the European Powers must not attempt colonization again.

James Monroe, the fifth US President and fourth from Virginia, died in 1831.

William Henry Harrison Campaign Photo Op

Photo by the Opposition

"Give him a barrel of hard cider and settle a pension ... on him, and ... he will sit the remainder of his days in his log cabin." Thus the supporters of Martin Van Buren's 1840 re-election assured their candidate's defeat. The Democrat in the White House was already perceived as being snobbish and elitist, so the Whigs contrasted their candidate as being not only a hero, which he certainly was, but a common man of the people, which he definitely was not.

Born at Berkeley Plantation in 1773, William Henry Harrison led a life of wealth and privilege. He went to Hampden-Sydney College and afterward began studies to become a doctor, but suddenly opted to join the army.

Sent to the all-but-unexplored Northwest, he earned fame at the Battle of Tippecanoe as a great Indian fighter, pushing the natives back from Ohio and Indiana. He also governed Indiana Territory and fought the combined British and Indian forces in the War of 1812, after which he returned to civilian life.

In 1840, "Old Tip" or "Tippecanoe" was elected the ninth President (fifth from Virginia). He was also the oldest man elected President in the 19th century, the first to die in office, and the President who, at one month, served the shortest time in office, dying of pneumonia he contracted at his cold, snowy inauguration.

"and Tyler Too!"

First US President to inherit the job after the elected President died, John Tyler was belittled as "His Accidency."

Born in 1790, he attended the College of William & Mary, studied law, and served two terms as US Congressman. He believed in strict adherence to the Constitution and voted against legislation promoting nationalism over states' rights. After serving two terms as Governor, he was elected Senator and joined the states' righters in opposing President Jackson. As running mates, Whigs William Henry Harrison and John Tyler used "Tippecanoe and Tyler Too" as their slogan.

Harrison died almost immediately after taking office, and Tyler became the tenth man (sixth from Virginia) to hold the office. His friends, as well as his opponents, were stunned when he acted just like a "real" President and fought hard for his beliefs, in spite of the fact he became President because of pure "luck". The Whigs kicked him out of their party, most of his cabinet resigned, and a resolution of impeachment (the first) was presented to the House, but failed to pass.

The political factions were regionally split, and Tyler's staunch defense of states' rights widened the gulf, but his stand made the Presidency stronger overall.

He died in 1862 while serving in the Confederate States' House of Representatives, and lies buried in Richmond's Hollywood Cemetery near James Monroe, who predeceased him.

Sam Houston

Fred Fort Worth

Jose El Paso

Stephen Austin

Virginia's Runaways to Texas

Numerous Virginians have "gone to Texas," of whom two became central to the founding of Texas as an independent entity and later, a US state. One was Sam Houston (1793-1863) born near Lexington, but lived most of his youth in Tennessee.

When war with Britain broke out in 1812, he enlisted in the army and served valiantly, was wounded, and left the service as a first lieutenant in 1818 to become a lawyer.

He found it easy to win election to political office, first in Tennessee, then in Texas. During his career he was a US Senator, governor of both states, and President of the Republic of Texas. As leader of the Anglo-Texan forces, he defeated General Santa Ana at the Battle of San Jacinto.

The other Virginian, born in Wythe County, Stephen Austin (1793-1836), spent all of his short adult life trying to get Anglo citizens of the US to colonize on lands in Mexican Texas and to get the Mexican government to treat them fairly according to agreements made along the way. Austin opposed the Texans' 1835 Declaration of Independence, but supported the Republic of Texas once the action had been taken, serving as Secretary of State until his death. The Texas state capital is named for him.

As for Jose El Paso and Fred Fort Worth, the author is unable to find any historical evidence of either. Ask the illustrator, and good luck!

Old Rough and Ready Zachary Taylor

Born in 1784 in Orange County, Zachary Taylor was a military hero in the Mexican War, a career officer in the US Army, and the 12th President of the United States (the 7th from Virginia).

As an infant, he moved with his family to Kentucky where he was brought up. He spent most of his army life on the frontier, managing the "Indian problem" for eastern politicians.

His command style was informal, but good enough to win battles at Monterrey and Buena Vista, and the soubriquet "Old Rough and Ready" from his troops. Though he owned a hundred slaves, lived in Louisiana, and owned land in Mississippi, he was not a devout Southern regionalist.

He was elected president at a time when politicos were wrangling with the question of slavery, and he came down firmly on the side of not spreading the practice to new territories, threatening to hang those who would rebel against the Union.

He died suddenly after a July 4th celebration, the second president to die in office.

Movin' the capitol from the big city of Williamsburg to here?

City folk sure are hard to figure, I say.

Richmond has a varied and extreme history, from the best of times to the worst of times and back again.

At present there are few indications of how the Native Americans lived in this area, but evidence shows there were ancient fishing villages here along the river. Fish swimming upstream to spawn were harvested at the base of the falls, easy prey for man and beast.

English settlers began a tiny settlement called "Henricus" near the falls and became the site of the first hospital in North America and the village in which Pocahontas was a captive for a while. Here she met her future husband, John Rolfe.

With the tobacco Rolfe developed bringing in good returns when sold in England, Henricus prospered until that awful morning in 1622 when the Powhatan people attacked all the English except at Jamestown and killed almost everybody.

In 1646, a treaty was signed which ceded to the English all the lands below the Falls on the James, but there remained continual friction along the frontier. At that time, Henrico included all the lands of present-day Henrico, Charles City, Powhatan, Chesterfield, and Goochland counties.

Then in the middle of the Revolution, the Capital of Virginia was moved to Richmond, home to a couple hundred people. Undefended, the town was burned by troops commanded by Benedict Arnold after Governor Jefferson refused to let English ships sail up to Richmond and empty the town's tobacco warehouses.

A much larger Richmond was burned in 1865 as retreating Confederates set fire to supplies they could not remove, thus to forbid them to approaching Union troops. The day is remembered as "Evacuation Sunday," as residents withdrew from the city ahead of the spreading flames. As seen in Matthew Brady's historic photographs, most of the city was left in ruins, desolate.

The Yankees, of course, were bent on taking Richmond because it had served as the Capital of the rebel states. There had dwelled Jefferson Davis and the Confederate Congress and Cabinet, who were long gone when the Union troops entered the town.

The "White House of the Confederacy" was not burned, nor was the Thomas Jefferson-designed Capitol, where even today sits the first and oldest legislature in the Western Hemisphere.

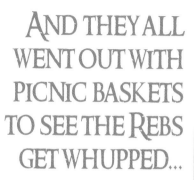

AND THEY ALL WENT OUT WITH PICNIC BASKETS TO SEE THE REBS GET WHUPPED...

It's July, 1861, Washington City is hot, and what could be more refreshing than riding out into the Virginia countryside to watch the army put an end to this war. We'll take a picnic lunch and watch those Secessioners get whipped! How thrilling!

And so, as the men in blue and the men in gray prepared to wage war against each other, carriages full of Washingtonians took positions for viewing the expected defeat of the Southern troops under General Beauregard. Upon the advance of General McDowell to Matthews Hill the battle started. In heavy fighting during most of the day, the Confederate forces were repeatedly driven back. At one point General Bee, trying:

a) to rally his troops to hold like those of General Jackson, or b) to complain of Jackson's lack of action, shouted, "There is Jackson standing like a stone wall!" Bee was killed within moments of the statement, but his words had given "Stonewall" Jackson the name by which he was soon known on both sides.

Late in the afternoon gray reinforcements arrived on a train and broke the Union advance. The Yanks' retreat degenerated into a rout and the road back to Washington became a dreadful traffic jam as soldiers competed with sightseers for space on the road to safety.

The tired and disorganized Rebs did not pursue them.

Andrew Sprowle acquired land along the southern branch of the Elizabeth River in 1767 and operated his profitable shipyard servicing Royal Navy vessels. When the Revolutionary War erupted and Lord Dunmore fled the Old Dominion, Sprowle went with him, sacrificing his "Gosport Navy Yard" and all his property to the new Commonwealth of Virginia, which had the largest navy of all the states.

As the US Navy's oldest (even older than the US Navy), Norfolk Naval Shipyard has been responsible for many "firsts" and "mosts." Here was built the *USS Chesapeake*, sister to the *USS Constitution* and one of the first six ships constructed for the US Navy.

Started here in 1827 was one of but two drydocks in the US, and though unfinished, this one was placed into service in 1833 when the *USS Delaware* became the first ship to enter drydock in the United States.

The Civil War saw the retreating Union forces set fire to the yard, the stores, and the 11 ships within. One of those was the *USS Merrimac*, a 40-gun steam frigate, which burned to the waterline. She was raised, put into the drydock, and rebuilt as the CSS *Virginia*, the first ironclad in the world to see action.

Built here, the *USS Texas* was launched in 1892, the first battleship in the US Navy. In 1919, the collier *Jupiter* was converted to become the Navy's first aircraft carrier, the *USS Langley*. All this, before the Second World War!

Artist's rendering of Gosport Navy Yard

The "Barn Roof" meets The "Cheese Box"

On March 8, 1862, the Yankee Navy had the port of Hampton Roads blockaded, when down the Elizabeth River steamed a vessel of which they had never dreamt. The CSS *Virginia*, built on the hull of the *USS Merrimac*, entered the quiet harbor and changed naval warfare forever. Her sides plated with iron, she attacked the anchored Union ships with impunity. Down went the mighty *USS Cumberland*, and *Virginia* turned to the *USS Congress*, whose guns were unable to penetrate the Rebel ship's armor. Next day, the ironclad *USS Monitor* arrived to defend the pummeled US fleet. The *Monitor*, derided as a "cheesebox on a raft" because of its unusual, low-riding design, and the *Virginia*, a "floating barn roof," battled fiercely to a draw.

Upon hearing of the ironclads' duel, Great Britain, with the world's pre-eminent navy, immediately abandoned the building of wooden warships.

May 15, 1864, over 200 VMI cadets charged into battle across muddy ground so viscous that some had their boots pulled off their feet as they ran. Near a little town called New Market boys of 16 (some say 14) to 18 years faced Union cannons with courage that would have made veteran soldiers proud. Each year, they are ceremonially remembered by their successors.

Named by Thomas Jefferson in tribute to the 1775 battle at Lexington, MA, Lexington, VA is the seat of Rockbridge County. The area is famous as the site of Natural Bridge and two historic schools: Washington & Lee University (W&L) and Virginia Military Institute (VMI).

George Washington made a gift of $20,000 to a struggling school called Liberty Hall, and the trustees renamed the facility Washington College. The late commander of the Army of Northern Virginia, General Robert E. Lee, took the position of president of the college and was instrumental in bringing the law school here. His tenure cut short by his 1870 death, he and members of his family are interred at W&L.

The school's alumni include telejournalist Roger Mudd,

Assoc. Justice of the US Supreme Court Lewis Powell, the Rev. Pat Robertson, and author Tom Wolfe.

VMI, "The West Point of the South," was conceived for the providing of guards at the state arsenal at Lexington, and the education and discipline for its students, when it was founded in 1839. Among those who taught here was T. J. (later "Stonewall") Jackson who looked at all the VMI alumni in his midst before Chancellorsville and commented, "The Institute will be heard from today." He was later killed by his own pickets and was returned to VMI for burial. Sigma Nu, the nation's first honor fraternity, was founded here.

Famous attendees include Nobel Peace Prize winner Gen. George C. Marshall, and Gen. George S. Patton, Jr.

ABE · LINCOLN · TOURS · FORT · MONROE

Drawn from an actual photograph. Some changes have occured.

In 1609, Point Comfort was chosen as the Jamestown Colony's primary base of defense against the Spanish and a stockade named Fort Algernourne was built.

At the point in 1728, Fort George was constructed of brick, only to be destroyed by a hurricane in 1749. Old Point Comfort Lighthouse was erected there in 1802, and was captured and used as a watchtower by the British during the War of 1812. The lighthouse still stands.

Named after the 5th US President, Fort Monroe was completed in 1834, the largest stone fort ever built in the US, and the only currently active US fort encircled by a moat. It is a Registered National Landmark.

A 2nd Lieutenant of Engineers named Robert E. Lee was stationed there from 1831 to 1834 to build its fortifications, and those of Fort Wool in the Hampton Roads Channel.

It was never taken by the CSA but remained a US citadel. There, General Benjamin Butler ordered that slaves who made it to US lines would be held as "contraband" and not returned to their masters. Slaves flocked to the area.

After the war, captured Confederate President, Jefferson Davis, was imprisoned in the casemate at the fort (his cell is now a museum) for two years before his release.

"It is well that war is so terrible. We should grow too fond of it."

Thus Confederate General Robert E. Lee spoke as he watched the destruction of Union General Ambrose Burnsides' army while it tried to take Marye's (pronounced Marie's) Heights under withering fire from Lee's forces.

Having replaced General MacClelland as commander of the Army of the Potomac, Burnsides rushed to take Richmond late in 1862. His plan was to move through Fredericksburg with relative ease and on to Richmond before winter set in, but was delayed by having to wait for pontoons he ordered to build bridges over the Rappahannock River.

The pontoons arrived and work began, but the Rebs fired with deadly aim from the town. After laying down a two-hour cannonade that destroyed the city, the Yanks were still under heavy fire, and had to proceed street by street once they rowed themselves across the broad expanse of deep water in the ungainly pontoons.

The battle ebbed and flowed for weeks until the armies faced each other across a wide sloping field on 13 December. At the top of the rise was a road, sunken below ground level by long years of use, and a stone wall from behind which the men of Lee's command sent a hailstorm of continual fire down upon the blue waves as they came, one after another, nine divisions in all. Not one Union soldier had touched the wall when the battle ended.

Petersburg Under Siege

Near the falls of the Appomattox River, Fort Henry was built in 1645 to guard the frontier. During the Revolution, the British occupied the town after defeating a much smaller militia force at Blandford, April 25, 1781, six months before the surrender at Yorktown.

After the war, the city grew, eventually became a railroad center, and thus a prime target for Union forces when the Civil War raged in the area. Petersburg's greatest historical claim is that it is the place wherein the longest siege in US history occurred, and within it, the Battle of the Crater.

Confederates held Petersburg as Federal forces arrived, June 15, 1864. Battles and skirmishes occurred almost daily at various places in the vicinity, and both sides received reinforcements. Frustrated at being so close and yet so far from their objective, one Northern command began tunneling under the Southern positions along their front. After about a month of digging, they packed the tunnel's farthest end with explosives and waited for orders to set it off.

Early on the morning of July 30, a horrendous blast erupted, creating a hole 500 feet across. The Union troops rushed into the depression to take the stunned Rebels. Fighting continued until early afternoon, when the recovered Confederates had captured many Federal troops.

All through the winter, the two sides battled with no real progress until April 2, 1865, when Lee withdrew his forces and headed west, toward Appomattox.

Wilmer couldn't run far enough...

After the Battle of First Bull Run, or First Manassas if you prefer, which raged across his farm on July 21, 1861, Wilmer McLean realized that the same lands would likely be fought over again, and moved his family to a place he thought would be farther from the dangers of the war.

Thus it was that, on April 9, 1865, generals Robert E. Lee and Ulysses S. Grant met at Appomattox Courthouse in Wilmer McLean's parlor and agreed to end the fighting between their forces.

After his surrender, Lee was offered grand sums of money to allow his name to be used in one commercial enterprize or another, but he refused. Instead he became president of Washington College, now Washington & Lee University, Lexington, where he died and was buried in 1870.

Next election after the war, Grant was voted in as President of the United States and served two terms, though he proved a better general than he was a president. He died in 1885 after finishing his memoirs, and is buried in NYC.

Arlington National Cemetery Stolen!

Mary Custis Lee, wife of Robert E. Lee, had inherited Arlington House, from her grandfather who built it. He was the grandson of Martha Custis Washington, and the much-loved adopted son of the first President.

While her husband commanded the Confederate Army of Northern Virginia, Mrs. Lee's home was taken by Union forces.

The war fatalities mounted, including that of the son of Union Quartermaster General Montgomery Meigs, who chose Arlington House as his site for revenge upon the Confederate general, and had 26 Union dead buried "in Mrs. Lee's rose garden." Those few were followed by thousands.

After the war, Mrs. Lee tried to return to her family home, but was not allowed to do so by the US, which claimed she had not paid the taxes on the home during the war. However, she had proof that she had tried to pay them and the taxes were refused, and so took the US government to court. A prolonged legal battle ensued that lasted many years. Mrs. Lee had died by the time the Supreme Court decided in her favor and ordered the US to pay her heirs for the illegally held property, hallowed ground now known to us as Arlington National Cemetery.

I DID PAY THE TAXES!!

Foreclosure

FROM SLAVE TO PRESIDENT

Born a slave in Franklin County in 1856, on a 200-acre tobacco farm, the boy who would call himself Booker T. Washington found that education was forbidden to him, but to school he was sent... to carry the books of his owner's child. He thought that to "get into a schoolhouse and study would be about the same as getting into paradise."

After the slaves were freed he and his family went to West Virginia to live with his step-father. There he worked in a salt mine and later as a houseboy, and went to school until he was 16 years old.

It was then that he left home and walked almost all of the 500 miles to Hampton Institute, a new school established just for blacks. Poorly clad and poorly trained, he had to prove himself to be admitted to the college, but once accepted, he worked his way through and became a teacher there.

He went on to found and serve as president of another school for black students, this one in Alabama, the Tuskegee Institute (famed for training the all-black fighter squadron of World War II, the Tuskegee Airmen).

"From the time that I can remember anything, almost every day of my life has been occupied in some kind of labor," he wrote. But his tireless works helped former slaves and their children achieve the dignity and opportunities afforded other Americans. He died, world renowned, in 1915.

A "GIRL" & A "LADY"

Born in Danville into post-Civil War privation and southern traditions, the five daughters of railroad tycoon Chiswell D. Langhorne became world famous for their beauty.

When Irene debuted in society, she went to NY for the Debutantes' Ball, the first southern belle to do so after the war. There she met and married the famous artist Charles Dana Gibson. Irene personified his idealized "Gibson Girl", and she became his frequent model.

Nancy and Phyllis also went North and married millionaires, but both divorced and moved to England. The sisters took Edwardian society by storm with their horsemanship and charm, as well as their loveliness and intellect.

Both married Englishmen. Nancy wed Waldorf Astor, Member of Parliament and heir to perhaps the world's largest fortune of the era. At his father's demise he also inherited his father's title (Viscount) and seat in the House of Lords, so Nancy ran for and won his vacated seat in the House of Commons, becoming the first woman in England's history to sit as a Member of Parliament, a position she held from 1919 to 1945.

Nancy Langhorne, Lady Astor succumbed in 1964.

Many stories circulated about her wit and humor, some true, some not, but a favorite is this: a supporter of Winston Churchill, Lady Astor is said to have gibed, "Winston, if I were your wife I would flavor your drink with poison," to which he growled, "If I were your husband, Madam, I should drink it!"

ol' 97

A locomotive pulling four cars made up the train engineered by Joseph Brody (or Broady), who realized that the air brakes would not hold while they were rushing downhill on a three-mile grade near Danville. He reversed the engine in a vain attempt to lock the wheels and slow his runaway, but approaching a curve before a high trestle, it tore up the tracks and sailed through the air, coming to rest 75 feet below at the base of the trestle. Brody and his firemen and nine others were killed.

When the song was recorded by Vernon Dalhart, a well-known light-opera singer, it became the first recording to sell a million copies. Thirty years after the wreck, the song was involved in the first major copyright suit: David A. George's claim of authorship was upheld by the court and he was awarded $65,000 for sales of 5 million records, but RCA kept the suit in the courts, and he never collected his award.

"The Wreck of the Old 97" is a simple ballad about a real tragedy near Danville on September 28, 1903.

As the song tells the tale, a mail train, Number 97 on the Southern Railway, had a run to Spencer, NC, from Monroe, VA. Just as in the ballad "Casey Jones," based on a train wreck some years before, Number 97 was running late and the engineer was told he had to be on time.

Just a hoot and a holler...

… from the Blue Ridge Parkway in Floyd County is a mill built by Edwin B. Mabry between 1903 and 1910, an era when most mountain folk had to grow or make everything they used... excepting sewing needles and coffee. Now considered quaint and peaceful, the mill was where people from miles around brought their grain to be ground into flour or meal and catch up on the news.

First constructed as a blacksmith's and wheelwright's shop, it was also a sawmill before becoming a grist mill. We often forget that water power would do so many things, but Mabry also had lathes, a jigsaw, and a planer in his mill. He built furniture and about anything else he needed.

If not the most photographed scene in the US, Mabry Mill is one of them. Yep, little Mabry Mill! Here visitors can also see how the miller and many of his mountain neighbors lived and worked, with walking trails and live demonstrations of tanning, smithing, shoemaking, and other crafts.

OUR VICTORY ARCH

Hampton Roads was the embarkation point for men and women going to three wars: the Spanish-American War and World Wars One and Two.

When it was over "over there" after the First World War, the people of the Peninsula constructed a wood and plaster "Victory Arch" under which they would welcome home the "doughboys." Tens of thousands of returning servicemen marched beneath its elaborate bend, which was dedicated five months after the Armistice. The "War to End All Wars" was won.

But that was a lie. It didn't end all wars. The next generation of American sons and daughters went "over there" to fight the Second World War, and many of them left through here. Between June 15, 1942, and September 1, 1945, 1,667,000 military service members passed through Hampton Roads Embarkation Point. Most of them returned to be welcomed by the Victory Arch.

By 1960, however, the original arch was no longer viable and was replaced by a permanent stone Victory Arch that stands in Newport News, today.

WOODROW WILSON

A World of Trouble, a World of Peace.

Woodrow Wilson was the 8th, and only 20th century, US President from Virginia. A native of Staunton, he was the son of a Presbyterian minister and educator in the South of the Reconstruction Era.

Born to be an academic, Wilson graduated from the College of New Jersey (Princeton) and the University of Virginia School of Law before matriculating to Johns Hopkins University for his doctorate.

In 1885 he married his first wife, and his career progressed quickly. Bright, conservative, a political science professor, he was soon the president of Princeton. Politicos began to notice, and he ran for the governorship of New Jersey in 1910 and won.

Two years later the Democrats ran him for president with a platform of states' rights and individualism, and again, he won. But during his 2nd term, he was no longer able to prevent the US' involvement in "Europe's War," and Congress declared war in 1917.

In a speech before Congress the next year, Wilson proposed a 14-point plan for enduring peace, the last of which was for an international organization that would evolve into the League of Nations, and went to Paris after the Armistice to try and get his plan for world peace accepted. He convinced everyone but Congress, which rejected the Versailles Treaty.

Traveling the country to promote it, Wilson suffered a stroke which left him enfeebled until his death in 1924. However, for his efforts, he was awarded the Nobel Peace Prize in 1919.

When construction started on the Blue Ridge Parkway, the country was in a Depression and it was conceived as a "make-work" project to aid unemployed architects and engineers. In the meantime, it gave paying jobs to numerous men with little or no education.

Started earlier was the shorter, and sooner to be finished, Skyline Drive which would run 105 miles through Shenandoah National Park, from Front Royal to Rockfish Gap. The Blue Ridge Parkway, however, would stretch 469 miles along the crests of the Appalachians (pronounced Apple-latch'ns) from the south end of the Skyline Drive, through the newly opened Great Smokey Mountains National Park in North Carolina.

Actual construction began in 1935 after a two-year planning stage. There was a delay during World War II but work continued afterward, until the only link left in the chain was a jog around Grandfather Mountain at Linville, NC. Fifty-two years after the first shovel-full of dirt was moved, the Parkway was dedicated.

From an altitude of 6,000 feet at an overlook in NC, to one of but 600 feet near the James River in VA, the scenic highway included 26 tunnels, 200 overlooks and parking areas, and dozens of bridges of various sizes. In many of the mountainous counties it ran through, the Skyline Drive was the very first paved road.

BLUE RIDGE PARKWAY HELPS DRIVE THE NATION

The Family Business

Since Colonial times, the forests and ridges of the eastern mountains have held stills and willing hands to work them. The denizens of the hills and hollers had to produce what they needed and wanted, and that included alcohol. When the Federal government put taxes on liquor in 1794, distillers in western Pennsylvania rebelled, and President George Washington himself led 13,000 troops to put the quietus on the revolt.

During "Reconstruction" after the Civil War, heavy tariffs were applied to most everything the South could produce and sell. A farmer couldn't grow and ship his tariffed corn to market and make a profit, but he could make the corn into liquor and sell it for a high enough price to make real money!

The hills of Southwest Virginia were soon a torrent of untaxed liquor being hauled to cities like Baltimore, Richmond, and Washington, DC. Now, I don't know, but some folks say they still do.

BIG. The Pentagon, home of the US Defense Department, is BIG... said to be the biggest office building in the world. It is difficult to realize its size by seeing photos, so check this out: The Pentagon has the floor space of three Empire State Buildings or two Chicago Merchandise Marts, and the whole US Capitol would fit into just one of its five sides.

Constructed in the early days of World War II, it took only 16 months to complete, with over 17 miles of corridors and 3.7 million square feet of office space. It now boasts 100 thousand miles of phone cable. It is serviced by one of the country's newest subways as well as bus lines and private autos.

To build here, swamps and dumps were turned into hundreds of acres of building site by filling them with 5.5 million cubic yards of earth. The building itself required 680,000 tons of dredged sand and gravel to mix 435,000 cubic yards of concrete. When it opened in January, 1943, it replaced 17 War Department office buildings.

With sadness, we will remember too, that here at the west wall, the third of the four jets flown by the terrorists crashed into the Pentagon, martyring 184 innocent Americans.

Nine months later, the damage repairs were complete and a memorial capsule was placed into the wall behind a fire-blackened block of limestone simply etched with "September 11, 2001."

Douglas MacArthur would have been a Virginian ...if his mother had not been out-of-town at the time

Norfolk's 1850 courthouse is recognized as a Virginia Historic Landmark and a National Historic Place. More than that, it is the final resting place of General of the Army (five-stars) Douglas MacArthur and his wife, Jean, and a memorial and museum displaying his personal papers and items, from the famous corncob pipes to his 1950 Chrysler Imperial.

Though he was born on an army base in Little Rock, AR, in 1880, MacArthur sometimes claimed that he would have been born in Norfolk, but his mother (a Norfolk native) was out of town at the time. He gifted his personal items to his adopted hometown in 1961, and the city responded with the impressive MacArthur Square.

Like his father, Arthur MacArthur, he was awarded the Congressional Medal of Honor. It, as well as the other military awards and memorabilia from his years as hero to the Philipines as well as the US, are displayed in Norfolk's MacArthur Memorial. Who could ever forget his famous promise to the Philipino people as he was ordered to leave the islands ahead of the Japanese invaders: "I shall return!"

The photos of his return, wading through the surf in the tropical sun, his aides accompanying him, are among the 86,000 photos and over two million letters and other documents held in the museum's collection.

Monument Avenue

"America's Most Beautiful Boulevard" as some call it, Monument Avenue in Richmond is a National Historic Landmark, the only street in the US to be so designated.

Originally an extension of Franklin Street, Monument Avenue was first endowed with statuary in 1890 with the official dedication of the bronze of General Robert E. Lee, distinguished as the only man in history to have been offered command of two opposing armies. But it was not until 1906 that the street got its name.

Traversing Richmond's renowned Fan District, the broad, tree-lined boulevard runs east and west through the city, its ample median interrupted with six heroic statues of Southerners, all but one Virginians, who captured Richmonders' hearts and imaginations as well as their own places in history.

In addition to Lee at Allen Street are: General Thomas J. "Stonewall" Jackson, at Boulevard; Matthew Fontaine Maury (called the "Pathfinder of the Sea" because of his scientific research of the oceans), at Belmont Avenue; Confederate President Jefferson Davis, the lone non-Virginian, at Davis Avenue; General J.E.B. Stuart, brilliant cavalry strategist, at Lombardy Street; and the most recent addition, international tennis star and Aids activist, Richmond native Arthur Ashe at Roseneath Road.

People come from all over the country and other lands to drive Richmond's most famous thoroughfare.

Another "must see" is the equestrian statue of Washington on the grounds of the Virginia Capitol

WISCONSIN IN VIRGINIA

Built at the Philadelphia Naval Yard and commissioned the first of three times on April 16, 1944, *USS Wisconsin*, BB 64, served her country in three conflicts: World War II (Leyte Gulf, Luzon, Iwo Jima, Okinawa, and the Japanese home islands), the Korean War (Kasong-Kosong, Kojo, Wonsan, Pusan, Hodo Pando, and Songjin), and the First Gulf War.

The only time the *Wisconsin* took a direct hit was in action at Songjin. She returned fire with effect.

Returning from having been decommissioned for a generation, the *USS Wisconsin* participated in Operation Desert Storm, part of the time in mine-laced waters, firing 16-inch rounds as well as Tomahawk missiles and other weapons in 36 separate naval gunfire support missions, the last on February 28, 1991.

The US Navy's last and biggest battleship, she now resides in her long-time home port of Norfolk, where she is a breath-taking floating museum at the National Maritime Center, Nauticus.

HELLO DOWN THERE

64

SURE TAKES MY BREATH AWAY

IM GITTIN' A CRICK IN MY NECK

The First African-American Ever Elected Governor of a US State

Lawrence Douglas Wilder was the first African-American ever elected to the governorship of, not only Virginia, but any US state.

Born in Richmond in 1931, he attended the city's segregated public schools and furthered his education at Virginia Union University, then an all black institution in the north of Richmond.

He graduated in 1951 with a degree in Chemistry, then served in the Korean War, for which he was awarded a Bronze Star.

With his G.I. Bill he graduated in 1959 from Howard University School of Law in Washington, DC, and subsequently founded the law firm of Wilder, Gregory & Associates in his home town. Ten years later, he won a special election and became the first African-American state senator in Virginia since Reconstruction, serving for a decade.

In the mid-1980s, he was elected Lt. Governor and four years later, the Democrat was elected Governor and served one term, as restricted by law. Afterward he declared himself a political Independent.

He was elected in 2004 to be Mayor of the City of Richmond, a post he holds as of this writing.

Tangier Island was actually a scattering of islets in Chesapeake Bay, according to early Virginia records. John Smith named them "Russell Isles" after a man who was aboard his ship at the time he sighted them in 1608. Tangier or Tangier Island today is a clutch of three small islets twelve miles from the Eastern Shore.

The people on Tangier are all but totally descended from settlers who were here in colonial times. Most are named Crockett and of the Methodist faith. Thanks to the influx of comparative hordes of tourists every summer, and to television and radio, the otherwise isolated islanders speak a now disappearing dialect still reminiscent of their English ancestors' tongue.

Originally the islands were farmed, but in the1840s, the people here began earning their living on the bounty of the surrounding waters, primarily oysters and crabs. Discovered and adored by big cities in the northeast, Chesapeake Bay oysters and blue crabs grew in demand and the islanders quit growing crops and harvested only from the waters. Working "dead rise" boats are a common site.

To get to the island, it is necessary to take a relaxing hour-and-a-half boat ride from the Eastern Shore at Onancock, Virginia, or Crisfield, Maryland. At this writing, the ferries run between Memorial Day and October 15th. Wear good walking shoes, or come prepared to ride a bike or golf cart, for there are no other vehicles on the island.

Dead Rise in the Morning, critters take warning

IRMA SUE

THE BARTER THEATER IN ABINGDON

THIS'LL BE BETTER THAN CLARK GABLE, MA!

SURE, PA...

The Barter Theater gives a good show, as it has ever since its founding in 1933, during the deepest depths of the Great Depression. An actor named Robert Porterfield, a native of Southwest Virginia, found himself out of work then, and came "home" to perform. Folks didn't have a lot of cash, and if a patron didn't have the 35-cent admission price, he or she could barter for a ticket with foodstuffs, such as canned goods, or fresh garden veggies. In that way, the actors ate, and the patrons were entertained. Bet you think you never heard of any of them, but among the actors who honed their craft on the stage of the Barter were: Gregory Peck, Ernest Borgnine, Patricia Neal, and Hume Cronyn.

LOOK, NELL, TONIGHT WE SUP ON COQ AU 'SHINE!

All Mine and Otelia's

William "Billy" Mahone, born in 1826 at Monroe, in Southhampton County, was a graduate of VMI and became a visionary in how to run a railroad. A civil engineer, he was involved in constructing several lines, including the Orange & Alexandria and Norfolk & Petersburg; of this last one he became president. He married Otelia Butler and had 13 children; of whom three lived to adulthood.

Foreseeing the viability of establishing a rail link between Norfolk and Bristol, he put aside his vision and went into the Confederate army in 1861. He rose through the ranks, being promoted to Brigadier General by General Lee after Mahone's heroic efforts at the Battle of the Crater.

Returning to managing railroads, he achieved his pre-war vision by combining three roads into the Atlantic Mississippi & Ohio. Asked once by a reporter what AM&O stood for, he quipped, "All mine and Otelia's."

The AM&O fell into other hands after the financial crisis of 1873, becoming the Norfolk & Western, headquartered in Roanoke until recent times. The City of Roanoke has paid homage to its roots, converting the old N&W Freight Depot into the Virginia Museum of Transportation.

Got trains?

There's Gold in them there hills...

For somebody.

A man rode into Lynchburg one day in the 1820s and left a fortune valued at $10 million or more. And he left detailed instructions on where in Bedford County it can be found. Only thing is, the instructions are in code, and even today the code is just partially broken though professional cryptologists have tried for generations.

So, if you'd like to take a shot at finding the 2,921 lbs. of gold, not to mention the silver and gems, those ol' boys in Bedford County are willing to let you dig holes 'most everywhere.

Why, they'll prob'ly even rent you a shovel.

SHOVELS FOR RENT... $25 PER DAY
CODE SHEETS... $5 EACH
DIGGIN' RIGHTS... $100
(PUT DIRT BACK WHEN FINISHED)
I GET HALF OF ALL FINDS
** NO REFUNDS **

Just about everyone has had a fish or two in a bowl or home aquarium, but at the Virginia Marine Science Museum there's a granddaddy of a setup, with over 800 thousand gallons of aquaria and live creature habitats: sharks and horseshoe crabs, harbor seals and lookdowns, sea horses and river otters.

Virginia's largest aquarium, VMSM is the reality of a concept first proposed in 1973. Ground was broken a decade later, and has had several additions along the way. Today, it totals 120 thousand square feet of space on 45 acres, including an IMAX theater (watch out for the sharks!).

Located at the VMSM is the Virginia Aquarium Stranding Team, which is called out to effect rescue of marine creatures that are injured or stranded on shore. On average, the team has attended 100 animals a year since 1991, including harbor seals, harbor porpoises, bottlenose dolphins, humpback whales, and loggerhead and kemp's ridley sea turtles. In December 2004, the team returned a rescued animal to the sea from the Virginia shore for the first time.

VMSM also conducts tours at sea and along Owl Creek Marsh in which experienced and knowledgeable guides point out aquatic life and try, depending on the particular tour, to locate whales or dolphins or Tidewater shore life.

Who's watching whom?

THE CHRYSLER MUSEUM HAS ART STUFF

This isn't going to be another one of those "china shop moments", is it Frank?

World's Best Tiffany Collection

Named for its greatest benefactor, "The Chrysler" was founded in 1939 as the Norfolk Museum of Arts and Sciences. The modest little facility set in downtown Norfolk had some very nice pieces, from ancient Egyptian and Greek sculpture to modern works by mostly mid-level artists. Then in 1971 Walter P. Chrysler, Jr., an heir to the Chrysler automobile family's fortune, donated his personal wide-ranging collection and the funds to enable the museum to expand.

Others have also donated pieces and collections to the repository, and its holdings and its stature have grown in recent years. Housing one of the world's finest collections of decorative glass, especially Tiffany, Steuben, and Quezal, as well as paintings by Cassatt, Rubens, Copley, Homer, Gainsborough, Van Dyke, Degas, Gauguin, O'Keefe, Renoir, and others, The Chrysler is today recognized as being among the best.

THE WAR MUSEUM HAS WAR STUFF

In honor of those who have fought for us throughout our history, the Virginia War Museum holds fascinating and rare artifacts to show us how they lived and fought. Here are relics from 1775 to our latest: weapons and uniforms, vehicles, insignia, propaganda posters, photos, histories, and more.

Here is a piece of an outer wall of Dachau, one of the Nazis' infamous concentration camps of WWII. Here is a section of the Communists' great failure, the Berlin Wall, and photos of those who built it... and of those who brought it down. Our conflicts, and our history.

THE MARINERS' MUSEUM HAS SEA STUFF

Virginia has always had her mariners. From Christopher Newport, who led the three ships that landed here in 1607, to today's seafarers, Virginia has always depended on those who go to sea, in war or in peace. It is thus appropriate that The Mariners' Museum, preserving and exhibiting seafarers' relics and histories, is located here, in Newport News.

Among its treasures: *USS Monitor* artifacts retrieved from the ocean's floor, ships' figureheads, amazingly detailed models of historic ships, small craft, ships' lists of immigrants from Jamestown to now, and more.

Virginia has a number of active zoos, including several that are participating in Species Survival Plans. Natural Bridge Zoo, which has dromedaries and white tigers, Mill Mountain Zoo at Roanoke (did you ever see snow leopards, or Red Pandas?), and the Virginia Zoological Park at Norfolk (the Virginia Zoo), all have endangered species in their care. At the Virginia Zoo, for instance, are African elephants and Bengal tigers and white Rhinos.

In addition, there is a wildlife habitat area at Busch Gardens in Williamsburg, and all sorts of bird and wildlife sanctuaries, from the islands off the eastern shore to the mountains on Virginia's western borders. Even some urban neighborhoods have been declared bird sanctuaries.

In recent decades, Virginia has engaged in an effort to repopulate her wilderness areas in species that were native to this region but were driven off or killed by the encroachment of people. Once great herds of buffalo and elk roamed the fields and forests here. Elk have been reintroduced on a small scale, as have their natural enemies, the wolves. Black bears and Virginia deer are still rather plentiful in the heavily wooded mountains and dense swamplands, but always remember that wild animals are not pets. Our zoos are the best places to observe them.

NOW, YOU'RE SPEAKING **MY** LANGUAGE

Who blew out the candle?

The mountains of western Virginia and her near neighbors are full of caverns and caves of various kinds, formed over eons by the constant dripping of mineral-bearing waters. Some of the formations are in such interesting colors and designs they have been named, such as Endless Caverns' "Bacon Strips", Dixie Caverns' "Turkey Wing", and Shenandoah Caverns' "Diamond Cascade." They really look like their names!

The largest caverns in the whole eastern half of the US are Luray Caverns, in Page County east of New Market. There, among other sights, you can see and hear the world's largest musical instrument, a Stalactite Organ, played on a regular organ keyboard, but covering over three-and-a-half acres, all underground! The notes are sounded by rubber mallets striking specially selected stalactites, each with its own musical tone. The mallets are activated by the corresponding key being played on the keyboard. Fascinating!

How do you remember which is a stalagmite and which a stalactite? Because the stalactite has to hold tight to the ceiling to keep from falling! The stalagmite is already attached to the ground.

No matter which of our caverns you visit, be sure and bring a sweater. It's a little cool down there at a constant 54 degrees!

Assateague to Chincoteague and Back

Off the quaintly beautiful Eastern Shore lie islands with unique qualities found nowhere else in the region. One has become world famous because of its wild horses. The romantic legend is that the small horses on Assateague are descendants of horses that were shipwrecked on Spanish vessels in the late 1500s or early 1600s. It's possible.

Also possible is that they descend from horses put on the island by colonists trying to hide them from the tax collector, since horses were taxed. Either way, the horses (they are not ponies) survive as they have for hundreds of years on the tough, salty grasses and shrubs of the dunes. Hence their small size.

Virginia's herd (there's one on Maryland's side of the island, too) is managed by the Chincoteague Volunteer Fire Department, which sees to the horses' overall health and hoof maintenance.

On the last Wednesday and Thursday of July every year, as they have since 1928, the Fire Department's "salt water cowboys" round up the horses and swim them across to the neighboring island of Chincoteague. There the foals are auctioned, but only to those who come equipped to transport and care for their horses. The annual sale keeps the herd from outgrowing the island's resources and helps support the Volunteer Fire Department, too!

Take all the photographs you like, but visitors to Assateague are asked not to feed or pet the horses because it draws them dangerously near to traffic.

NATIONAL
D-DAY
MEMORIAL

On a hilltop in Bedford County is a black and white and gray stone arch named "Overlord." It stands exactly 44' 6" above the surrounding memorial, those numbers commemorating the date June 06, 1944, D-Day, when forces from 12 nations stormed the Nazi-held beaches called Omaha, Utah, Gold, Sword, and Juno.

In three separate but linked areas, the site includes the "English Garden", a floral tribute laid out in the shape of the SHAEF (Supreme Headquarters Allied Expeditionary Force) shoulder patch, representing the planning and preparations for the invasion; the middle plaza, symbolizing the assault on the beaches and cliffs, with bronze sculptures of American troops wading ashore through gunfire; the top plaza standing for Victory and its cost, eloquently shown in a sculpture of a rifle stuck in the ground by its bayonet, and topped by a G.I.'s helmet.

Why was the National D-Day Memorial built here, in this small town? Because it is appropriate that we remember that 19 men of little Bedford were killed on June 06, 1944 ...more, for its size, than were lost by any other US community.

And here we remember, by name, all 4,500 men of the Allies' forces who died in the invasion that one day.

"Uncommon Valor..."

We have our share of monuments and statues and other memorials within the Commonwealth, but none deserves more honor than the one that stands outside of Washington, DC, in Northern Virginia. It's a bronze sculpture adapted from a World War II photo of five US Marines implanting a flag on top of Mount Suribachi, Iwo Jima, February 23, 1945. After the costly battle for the tiny island, Admiral Chester W. Nimitz so admired the Marines' courageous victory that he said of them, "Uncommon Valor was a Common Virtue".

Not far from the Pentagon in Northern Virginia, the heart-swelling bronze on its granite base is a national tribute to Marines who, since 1775, have paid for our freedom with their lives on the battlefields of the world. Marines, their families and friends, and Navy personnel paid for the magnificent work.

It stands 78 feet in height, and the 32-foot high figures strain to put up a 60-foot bronze flagpole on which, by presidential proclamation, flies a cloth US flag 24 hours a day.

We are proud to be the home of the US Marine Corps War Memorial. Thanks, Marines.

Ah! The Homestead.

Sam Snead started caddying here as a boy in 1919 and in 1934 became the first golf professional at the Cascades Course.

As early as the 1720s, explorers and surveyors had discovered the many mineral springs of the Virginia Highlands. Among them were the hot and warm springs in today's Bath County, and one of those early visitors, about 1755, was a young militia officer named George Washington.

A fellow militiaman, John Bullett, would acquire some of the region's best springs, build a rustic lodge on the site, and establish The Homestead, such as it was, about 1766. People came to "take the waters," since drinking and bathing in the naturally heated mineral waters were thought to be healthful.

Purchased by Dr. Thomas Goode in the 1830s, the rustic resort became more sophisticated, more like the European spas, and quite fashionable. 'Twas a great gathering place for those in high society. Notables and the powerful, trying to relax and escape the summer's heat, flocked to the elegant hotel in the cool Virginia mountains to socialize in the warm pool for men, and later, one for women. Then, of course, there was golf. An eight-hole course was built, and its First Tee is the oldest in continuous use in America.

Among those who tarried here: Thomas Edison, Jay P. Morgan (who bought the place), golfer Bobby Jones (who designed the Homestead's Third Course), industrialists, movie stars, and 22 US Presidents, 23 if we're counting that young militia officer.

When the new Moose Club (#733) down in Galax needed money to get up and running in the middle of the Deeeepression, they hit upon the idea of holding an Old Fiddler's Convention that Spring. It was a great success and enjoyed by everyone, so they set out to hold another one that Fall. It overflowed the facility and had to be moved outdoors to Felts Park where it's been ever since. Now the musicians, a few from the earliest days, play to SRO crowds from all over the world. Young'uns come to learn how to play like the Ol' Fiddlers (and pickers). It's held the second weekend in August. Y'all come!

"...For people of today to hear and enjoy the tunes of yesterday"

THE LEGEND OF THE FAIRY STONES

In the lush green mountains not far from the Blue Ridge Parkway in Patrick County, is a Virginia State Park called Fairystone. It is named for the legend of the Fairy Stones (Staurolite) once found there in abundance.

The legend is this: on the day Jesus was crucified, the angels in heaven were so distraught that they began to cry. They did not want God to see them crying, and so they flew to a far corner of heaven to weep. Their tears fell to earth in Patrick County* and wherever they landed, small crosses formed from the mixture of angel tears and earthly soil.

Fairy Stones are considered by many to bring good luck. In this region they are usually reddish brown to cocoa brown, and many form perfectly proportioned crosses either in the "t" shape or the "X", or St. Andrew's cross, shape. Years ago they could be easily picked up from the grounds within the park but are rarer now.

*Unlike what the author remembers from childhood, Fairy Stones are found in many colors and in other parts of the world. (Sigh)

family trees have deep roots in Virginia

Never ask a Virginian about genealogy unless you mean it! Oh, many of them will stare at you blankly, as if you had asked about quantum physics, but the rest will rattle off the begats of the generations preceding theirs, for as long as you are willing to listen.

People who thought history class was interminably boring can offer details about their ancestors' service in the Revolution as if they had been there.

We'll brag, not only about our children and our grands, but about our fathers and mothers and the events of their lives, the pride we take in their heroism and courage, their wisdom and their humor, their foibles, too.

There are Virginians hiding in the ancestry of unsuspecting families all across the country... even Yankees! ;-) And, yes, there may be a Virginian or two whose family trees' roots reach out to other states.

A charming Virginia woman told me about her child's new teacher, who asked the kids to bring some information on their families for history class. My friend printed out a family tree for her child to take to school. A few days later, the swamped teacher sent a note home with the kids to please stop sending in genealogical information, she was overwhelmed with data!

Life don't get no better than this...

The Blue Ridge Mountains are the jagged pale blue line one sees when heading west on the rolling landscape of the Piedmont of Virginia.

First visited and named by Governor Alexander Spotswood and his "Knights of the Golden Horseshoe" in 1716, and later divided from the mountains of NC by a group including Peter Jefferson, father of Thomas, the Blue Ridge heralds the approach of the eastern "Continental Divide." Highest point in Virginia, at 5,758 feet, is Mount Rogers in the Jefferson National Forest near Marion in the Appalachians.

Dr. Thomas Walker visited and mapped the western wilds as far as today's Kingsport, TN. Other explorers had roamed beyond the ridges and hollers of the Appalachians and excited interest in the likes of Daniel Boone, who explored a bit, too, in his day.

Early immigrants leaving the port of Philadelphia and heading west followed an old Indian trail that came to be called "The Great Philadelphia Wagon Road" or the "Carolina Road," mimicked today by US Route 11.

Tens of thousands of pioneers and immigrants headed off into the wilderness to settle in the beautiful mountains and valleys of Virginia (or the Carolinas, or Georgia and west and south). Particularly plentiful were the Germans, the "Ulster Scots" and the Scots, who, on reaching the rugged hills, thought they had come home again. Many a hardy mountain family descends from those earliest settlers.

Among Virginia's other "favorite sons" is a four-legged entry by the name of Secretariat, perhaps the greatest thoroughbred of all time.

Born at Doswell (north of Richmond) in 1970, the "Big Red Horse" stood 16'2 hands and weighed 1200 pounds. Chosen Horse of the Year as both a two- and three-year-old, he was also a Triple-Crown-Winner, setting records in each: Kentucky Derby, new track record; Preakness Stakes, new track record; Belmont Stakes, he set a new world record, coming in at 2:24 and leading the nearest competition by 31 lengths, all but unheard of in racing history! His record stands unbroken to this day. We'll never see his like again.

Secretariat in the Home Stretch Wins by 31 Lengths!

See ya!

HAVE A RIGHT GOOD-SIZED GOOBER PEA?

"Goodness how delicious, eating goober peas," went the old Civil War era song. This incredible edible is thought to have originated in Brazil or Peru, where pottery from around 3500 years ago is in the shape of, or decorated with, peanuts. Storage jars full of peanuts were ofttimes left in Incan tombs.

The plant spread northward as far as Mexico, from where the tasty morsels were taken to Spain by the Conquistadors. Africa was the next stop, as they were taken on Spanish ships for food. On their fourth continent they were cultivated, mostly in the western areas from where slaves were often taken by slavers.

It was the slaves who brought their "ngubas" (get it? Goobers... ngubas?) with them and first planted them in the southeastern US, where they thrived. Also called "groundnuts" "or groundpeas" the little munchies were found to be an excellent food... for pigs! (Ever heard of Virginia's "peanut-fed" hams? Yum!)

We don't know when the very first ones were grown in Virginia, but the first commercial crop was grown in Sussex around 1840. The Virginia peanut is unequivocally the biggest.

Civil War soldiers helped spread the snack's popularity, but not until around 1900 was the equipment developed to make them easier to pick and clean, thus making them more widely enjoyable and profitable.

Why do we call them peanuts? Because some clever ad-man somewhere didn't think "Goober Pea Butter" sounded too awfully good. Go figure. ;-}